A Parents Magazine
Read Aloud Original

Library of Congress Cataloging in Publication Data
Asch, Frank.
George's Store.
Adapted from McGraw-Hill edition, New York, 1969.
Summary: George and his parrot Pete are usually successful at
guessing what their customers want until the day an unusual lady
walks into their store.
[1. Stores, Retail—Fiction]   I. Wiseman, Bernard,
ill. II. Title.
PZ7.A778Ge   1983   [E]   82–22298
ISBN 0-8193-1101-4
ISBN 0-8193-1102-2   (lib. bdg.)

GEORGE'S STORE

Story by
Frank Asch

Pictures by B. Wiseman

Parents Magazine Press · New York

When George was a little boy
he lived with his mother and father
in the back of their grocery store.

Sometimes George helped in the store.
He swept the floor,
dusted the shelves...

and even waited on customers.

and even waited on customers.

So when George grew up...

he started a store of his own.

Every day when the floor had been swept
and the shelves had been dusted,
George and his pet parrot, Pete,
sat down to wait for customers.

Whenever a customer came in,
George and Pete played a game.
They tried to guess what
each person wanted to buy.

Then one day
a lady in a red dress
walked into George's Store.

George and Pete tried to
guess what she wanted.

A toy plane? A wind-up train? A weather vane? Plants? Ants? Pants? A drum? A plum? Some chewing gum?
No! No! No! No!

And so they were married.

And they raised a family.

And they all lived together
in the back of...

George's Store.

About the Author

FRANK ASCH is the award winning author/
artist of many well-loved picture books,
including SANDCAKE and POPCORN, which
are part of the Bear Story series he created
for Parents. Mr. Asch lives in Middletown
Springs, Vermont, with his wife, Jan, and son,
Devin, who loves playing store.

About the Artist

BERNARD WISEMAN was a *New Yorker*
cartoonist/idea man for many years. He left
cartooning to start a series of stories for
children that was syndicated in Sunday papers
nationwide and then turned to creating
children's books. Mr. Wiseman lives with his
wife and children in Florida. There is a store
just like George's nearby.